HORRiD HENRY'S
Stinkbomb

HORRiD HENRY'S
Stinkbomb

Francesca Simon
Illustrated by Tony Ross

Orion
Children's Books

ORION CHILDREN'S BOOKS

Horrid Henry's Stinkbomb first published in Great Britain in 2008
by Orion Children's Books
This edition first published in Great Britain in 2016
by Hodder and Stoughton

1 3 5 7 9 10 8 6 4 2

Text copyright © Francesca Simon, 2008
Illustrations copyright © Tony Ross, 2008, 2016

A CIP catalogue record for this book
is available from the British Library.

ISBN 978 1 4440 1604 8

Printed and bound in China

The paper and board used in this book are from well-managed forests
and other responsible sources.

Orion Children's Books
An imprint of
Hachette Children's Group
Part of Hodder and Stoughton
Carmelite House
50 Victoria Embankment
London EC4Y 0DZ

An Hachette UK Company
www.hachette.co.uk

www.hachettechildrens.co.uk

For Louis

There are many more
Horrid Henry Early Reader books available.

For a complete list visit:
www.horridhenry.co.uk
or
www.orionchildrensbooks.com

Contents

Chapter 1   11

Chapter 2   19

Chapter 3   27

Chapter 4   33

Chapter 5   43

Chapter 6   53

Chapter 7   61

Chapter 1

"I hate you, Margaret!"

shrieked Sour Susan.
She stumbled out of the
Secret Club tent.

"I hate you too!"
shrieked Moody Margaret.
Sour Susan stuck out her tongue.

Moody
Margaret stuck
out hers back.

"I quit!" yelled Susan.

"You can't quit.
You're fired!"
yelled Margaret.

"You can't fire me. I quit!"
said Susan.

"I fired you first," said Margaret.
"And I'm changing the password!"

"Go ahead. See if I care.
I don't want to be in the Secret
Club anymore!" said Susan sourly.

"Good!
Because we don't want you."

Moody Margaret flounced back
inside the Secret Club tent.

Sour Susan stalked off.
Free at last!
Susan was sick and tired of her
ex-best friend Bossyboots Margaret.

Blaming her for the disastrous raid
on the Purple Hand Fort when
it was all Margaret's fault was
bad enough.

But then to ask stupid Linda
to join the Secret Club
without even telling her!

Susan hated Linda even more
than she hated Margaret.
Linda hadn't invited Susan
to her sleepover party.

And she was a copycat.

But Margaret didn't care.
Today she'd made Linda chief spy.

Well, Susan had had enough.
Margaret had been mean to her
once too often.

Susan heard gales of laughter
from inside the club tent.
So they were laughing, were they?
Laughing at her, no doubt?

Well, she'd show them.

Chapter 2

Susan knew all about
Margaret's Top Secret Plans.
And she knew someone who
would be very interested in
that information.

"Halt! Password!"

"Smelly toads," said Perfect Peter.
He waited outside Henry's
Purple Hand Fort.

"Wrong," said Horrid Henry.

"What's the new one then?"
said Perfect Peter.

"I'm not telling you," said Henry.
"You're fired, remember?"

Perfect Peter did remember.
He had hoped Henry had forgotten.

"Can't I join again, Henry?"
asked Peter.

"No way!" said Horrid Henry.

"Please?" said Perfect Peter.

"No," said Horrid Henry.
"Ralph's taken over your duties."

Rude Ralph poked his head through
the branches of Henry's lair.

"No babies allowed,"
said Rude Ralph.

"We don't want you here, Peter,"
said Horrid Henry. "Get lost."

Perfect Peter burst into tears.

"Crybaby!" jeered Horrid Henry.

"Crybaby!" jeered Rude Ralph.

That did it.

"Mum!" wailed Perfect Peter.
He ran towards the house.
"Henry won't let me play
and he called me a crybaby!"

"Stop being horrid, Henry!"
shouted Mum.

Chapter 3

Peter waited.
Mum didn't say anything else.

Perfect Peter started to wail louder.
"Muuum!
Henry's being mean to me!"

"Leave Peter alone, Henry!" shouted
Mum. She came out of the house.
Her hands were covered in dough.

"Henry, if you don't stop—"
Mum looked around.
"Where's Henry?"

"In his fort," snivelled Peter.

"I thought you said he was being
mean to you," said Mum.

"He was!" wailed Peter.

"Just keep away from him,"
said Mum.
She went back into the house.

Perfect Peter was outraged.

Was that it?

Why hadn't she punished Henry?
Henry had been so horrid
he deserved to go to prison
for a year.

Two years.

And just get a crust of bread a week.
And brussel sprouts.

Ha!
That would serve Henry right.

But until Henry went to prison,
how could Peter pay him back?

And then Peter knew exactly
what he could do.
He checked carefully to see
that no one was watching.
Then he sneaked over the garden
wall and headed for the
Secret Club Tent.

Chapter 4

"He isn't!"
said Margaret.

"She wouldn't,"
said Henry.

"He's planning to swap our lemonade for a Dungeon Drink?" said Margaret.

"Yes," said Peter.

"She's planning to stinkbomb
The Purple Hand Fort?" said Henry.

"Yes," said Susan.

"How dare she?" said Henry.

"How dare he?"said Margaret.
"I'll easily put a stop to that. Linda!"
she barked. "Hide the lemonade!"
Linda yawned.

"Hide it yourself," she said.
"I'm tired."

Margaret glared at her, then hid
the jug under a box.

"Ha ha! Won't Henry be
shocked when he sneaks over and
there are no drinks to spike!"
gloated Margaret.

"Peter, you're a hero. I award you the Triple Star, the highest honour the Secret Club can bestow."

"Ooh, thanks!" said Peter.
It was nice being appreciated
for a change.

"So from now on,"
said Moody Margaret,
"you're working for me."

"Okay," said the traitor.

★

Horrid Henry rubbed his hands.
This was fantastic! At last he had
a spy in the enemy's camp!
He'd easily defend himself against
that stupid stinkbomb.

Margaret would only let it off
when he was in the fort.
His sentry would be on the lookout
armed with a goo-shooter.

When Margaret tried to sneak
in with her stinkbomb –

ker-pow!

"Hang on a sec," said Horrid Henry,
"why should I trust you?"

"Because
Margaret is mean
and horrible
and I hate her,"
said Susan.

"So from now on," said Horrid Henry, "you're working for me."

Susan wasn't sure she liked the sound of that. Then she remembered Margaret's mean cackle.

"Okay," said the traitor.

Chapter 5

Peter sneaked back into his garden
and collided with someone.

"Ouch!" said Peter.

"Watch where you're going!"
snapped Susan.

They glared at each other
suspiciously.

"What were you doing at Margaret's?" said Susan.

"Nothing," said Peter. "What were you doing at my house?"

"Nothing," said Susan.

Peter walked towards
Henry's fort, whistling.

Susan walked towards
Margaret's tent, whistling.

Well, if Susan was spying on
Henry for Margaret, Peter certainly
wasn't going to warn him.
Serve Henry right.

Well, if Peter was spying on
Margaret for Henry, Susan certainly
wasn't going to warn her.
Serve Margaret right.

Dungeon drinks, eh?
Margaret liked that idea much better
than her stinkbomb plot.

"I've changed my mind about the stinkbomb," said Margaret. "I'm going to swap his drinks for dungeon drink stinkers instead."

"Good idea," said Lazy Linda. "Less work."

Stinkbomb, eh?
Henry liked that much better
than his dungeon drink plot.
Why hadn't he thought of that
himself?

"I've changed my mind about the Dungeon Drinks," said Henry. "I'm going to stinkbomb her instead."

"Yeah," said Rude Ralph. "When?"

"Now," said Horrid Henry.
"Come on, let's go to my room."

Chapter 6

Horrid Henry opened his
Stinky Stinkbomb kit.

He'd bought it with Grandma.
Mum would never have let him
buy it. But because Grandma had
given him the money Mum couldn't
do anything about it. Ha ha ha.

Now, which pong would he pick?
He looked at the test tubes
filled with powder and read
the gruesome labels.

Bad breath.

Dog poo.

Rotten eggs.

Smelly socks.

Dead fish.

Sewer stench.

"I'd go for dead fish," said Ralph.
"That's the worst."

Henry considered.
"How about we mix dead fish
and rotten eggs?"

"Yeah," said Rude Ralph.

Slowly, carefully, Horrid Henry
measured out a teaspoon of
Dead Fish powder, and a teaspoon
of Rotten Egg powder, into the
special pouch.

Slowly, carefully, Rude Ralph
poured out 150 millilitres of secret
stinkbomb liquid into the bottle
and capped it tightly.

All they had to do was to add the
powder to the bottle outside the
Secret Club and—
run!

"Ready?" said Horrid Henry.

"Ready," said Rude Ralph.

"Whatever you do,"
said Horrid Henry, "don't spill it."

Chapter 7

"So you've come crawling back,"
said Moody Margaret.
"I knew you would."

"No," said Sour Susan.
"I just happened to be passing."

She looked around the
Secret Club Tent.
"Where's Linda?"

Margaret scowled. "Gone."

"Gone for today, or gone forever?"
said Susan.

"Forever," said Margaret savagely.
"I don't ever want to see that lazy
lump again."

Margaret and Susan looked
at each other.
Susan tapped her foot.
Margaret hummed.

"Well?" said Margaret.

"Well what?" said Susan.

"Are you rejoining the Secret Club as Chief Spy or aren't you?"

"I might," said Susan.
"And I might not."

"Suit yourself," said Margaret. "I'll call Gurinder and ask her to join instead."

"Okay," said Susan quickly. "I'll join."

Should she mention her visit to Henry? Better not. After all, what Margaret didn't know wouldn't hurt her.

"Now, about my stinkbomb plot,"
began Margaret. "I decided—"

Something shattered on the ground
inside the tent.

A ghastly, gruesome,
grisly stinky stench filled the air.

"**Aaaaarggggg!**"

screamed Margaret, gagging.

"It's a —**stinkbomb!**"

"Help!"

shrieked Sour Susan.

"Stinkbomb!

Help! Help!"

Victory!

Horrid Henry and Rude Ralph
ran back to the Purple Hand Fort
and rolled round the floor,
laughing and shrieking.

What a triumph!
Margaret and Susan screaming!

Margaret's mum screaming!

Margaret's dad screaming!

And the stink!

Wow!

Horrid Henry had never
smelled anything so awful in his life.
This called for a celebration.
Horrid Henry offered Ralph a fistful
of sweets and poured out two glasses
of Fizzywizz drinks.

"Cheers!" said Henry.

"Cheers!" said Ralph.

They drank.

"Aaaaaarrgggggg!"

choked Rude Ralph.

"Blecccccch!" yelped Horrid Henry,
gagging and spitting.
"We've been—" cough!—
"dungeon-drinked!"

And then Horrid Henry heard
a horrible sound.

Moody Margaret and Sour Susan
were outside the
Purple Hand Fort.
Chanting a victory chant:

"Nah nah ne
nah nah!"

What are you going to read next?

Have more adventures with Horrid Henry,

or save the day with Anthony Ant!

Become a superhero with Monstar,

float off to sea with Algy,

or have your very own Pirates' Picnic.

Grow carrots with

Lottie and Dottie,

make magic with The Witch Dog,

and cast a spell with The Three Little Magicians.

Enjoy all the Early Readers.